Guess Who My Favorite Person Is

by Byrd Baylor   illustrated by Robert Andrew Parker

Aladdin Books
Macmillan Publishing Company
New York

I happened
to be
in an alfalfa field,
barefoot,
sort of
lying down
watching
ladybugs
climb
yellow flowers
when
I saw
this little farm kid
who was also
barefoot,
sort of
lying down
watching
ladybugs
climb
yellow flowers,
helping them up again
when they fell off.

"Want to see
my favorite
one?"
she called to me.

So
I went over to
where she was.

She pointed to
a
bug.

To tell the truth,
I couldn't see
much difference between
that one
and about a million
others.

I was
going back
to my own
part
of the field
when she said,
"Now
choose
your
favorite one."

It wasn't easy
because
I hadn't ever
practiced
choosing
ladybugs
but
finally
I did.

She looked surprised.
"I can't believe
you like
that one.
I passed her up
about two days
ago…
but that's your
business."

For a while
we didn't
talk at all.

I stretched out
and closed my eyes
and just let
the alfalfa
be
taller
than
I was

but
she said,
"What's your favorite
thing—
sleeping
or being awake?"

"Awake,"
I said.

"Then wake up
and we can play
the
tell-what-your-favorite-thing-is
game."

"I think
we are
already
playing it,"
I said.

She said,
"We are,
and it's
my turn.
My favorite turn
is FIRST."

So I said,
"Go ahead."

She said,
"Tell
your favorite
color."

I said,
"Blue."

But
she said,
"See,
you've already
done it wrong.
In this game
you can't just say
it's blue.
You have to say
what *kind* of
blue."

So I said,
"All right.
You know
the
blue
on a lizard's
belly?
That sudden kind of
blue
you see
just
for a second
sometime—
so blue
that
afterwards
you always think
you made it up?"

"Sure,"
she said.
"I know that kind
of blue."

Then
she told me
hers
and it was
brown.

Maybe
I looked
surprised
because
she said,
"Not many people
appreciate
brown
but
I don't care.
I do.
And the one
I like the best
is
a dark reddish brown
that's
good
for mountains
and for rocks.
You see it
in steep cliffs
a lot."

I said,
"I know
that kind of brown."

Then it was
my turn
to ask
so
I said,
"What's your
favorite thing
to touch?"

She said,
"My feet
like
mud
but
my face
likes
wind,
especially
if I'm running up
a hill,
so I have to
choose
both things."

I said,
"Wait.
It isn't fair
to choose
two
favorite things."

"It is
when you have to,"
she said.
"Any other way
to play it
would be
silly."

I could see
that
she
was right.

I said
my favorite thing
to touch
was
kitten fur

but then
I changed my mind
and wanted
clear
creek water

and then
I changed again
and
that time
I was sure
my favorite thing
was
sand,
clean
dry
powdery
desert sand.

She didn't like it
that I changed
my mind
but
all she said was,
"It makes
the game
go better
if you've
already thought of
all your favorite things
before
you play."

I said
I would
next time.

Then
we chose
our favorite
sounds.

She said
hers was
bees
but not
just
one
or two.
She said
it takes
about
a thousand
bees
buzzing
in all the
fields
around
to make
the kind of
loud
bee sound
she likes.

For mine,
I chose
a bird
I'd heard
one morning
in the mountains
in New Mexico
and never
saw
and never
heard again
and couldn't
even say
why
I still
remember it.

She said
it was all right
that
I didn't know
its name.

So
we
went on to
what's your favorite
place to live.

She said
her favorite
place to live
was
in
a tree.

I said,
"Doesn't it have to be
someplace
you've
really lived?"

She said,
"That's right,
it does.
And
I've lived
in
lots
of trees."

She didn't say
how long she'd lived
in any tree
and
I
didn't
ask.

I said
I knew
my favorite place
to live
but

I wasn't sure
it was fair
to say
because
I hadn't
really
lived there
yet—
even though
I plan to.

She said
the rule is
that
it's okay
if
you're
pretty sure
you're
going
to live there
someday.

So
I said,
"I am.
It's
in
a cave
with foxes."

"That's
fair,"
she said.
"I think
a tree
is best
for summer
but
a cave
would be
all right
for
winter nights."

We must have
named
a hundred
favorite
things
that afternoon.

I remember
that
her favorite
dream
is
FLYING.
She said
it is so
easy
in that dream,
looking down
on little hills
and valleys,
flapping
her arms
when she wants
to go
higher.

She said
she'd dreamed it
seven times.

Mine is
finding
turquoise beads
when
I'm
just
walking along,
not
really
looking,
not trying to find them.

I dreamed it
once
about a year
ago.

Her favorite
thing
to see
moving
is
fish
underwater.

Mine
is
falling stars.

Her favorite
thing
to taste
is
snow
and honey mixed…
a little more
honey
than snow.

Mine
is
bread
just baked
at home,
still warm.

Her favorite
smell
is the
alfalfa
growing
in this field.

Mine is
desert rain—
not rain
anywhere
else.

Her favorite
shape
is zig-zag.

Mine
is
round.

Finally
I said,
"What's
your favorite
time of day?"

And
she said,
"Now,
just about
now
when
I've been
running
in the field
and getting
out of breath
and falling down
and watching ladybugs
and finding someone
to play
the tell-what-your-favorite-thing-is
game
and playing it
and then
maybe
walking back
as far as the road
together."

I wasn't sure
she'd
let us both
choose
the same thing
but
she was
nice
about it.

She said,
"We can.
That's
my favorite way
to end
the game."

By then
it was
getting
late
so
we walked
back
as far as
the road
together.

I was going to say
that
sunrise
is
my favorite
time of day

but
when
I thought about it
I wanted
to choose
now
too.

Byrd Baylor
is the author of many
distinguished books including
three Caldecott Honor Books—
When Clay Sings
illustrated by Tom Bahti,
and *The Desert Is Theirs*
and *Hawk, I'm Your Brother,*
both illustrated by Peter Parnall.
And It Is Still That Way
is a collection she has made
of legends told by
Arizona Indian children.
Ms. Baylor lives in
the Southwest.

Robert Andrew Parker
has illustrated many
outstanding children's books
including *The Trees Stand Shining,*
Poetry of the
North American Indians
selected by Hettie Jones,
and *Pop Corn and Ma Goodness*
by Edna Mitchell Preston,
a Caldecott Honor Book.
Mr. Parker lives in
New York State.

Aladdin Books
Macmillan Publishing Company
866 Third Avenue, New York, NY 10022
Collier Macmillan Canada, Inc.

First Aladdin Books edition 1985
Originally published by Charles Scribner's
Sons, Macmillan Publishing Company.
Printed in the United States of America

10 9 8 .7 6 5 4 3

**Library of Congress
Cataloging-in-Publication Data**

Baylor, Byrd.
   Guess who my favorite person is.

   Reprint. Originally published: New York:
Scribners, c1977.
   Summary: Two friends play the game of
naming their favorite things.
   [1. Play—Fiction] I. Parker, Robert Andrew, ill.
II. Title.
PZ7.B3435Gu 1985 [E] 86-22248
ISBN 0-689-71052-6 (pbk.)